W9-ARG-588

DISCARDED

Old MacDonald
Had a . . . ZOO?

*As told and
illustrated by*
Iza Trapani

Charlesbridge

To the Flavins, with a *cluck cluck* here and a
cluck cluck there and lots of love everywhere

Copyright © 2017 by Iza Trapani
All rights reserved, including the right of reproduction in whole or in part in any form.
Charlesbridge and colophon are registered trademarks of Charlesbridge Publishing, Inc.

Published by Charlesbridge
85 Main Street
Watertown, MA 02472
(617) 926-0329
www.charlesbridge.com

Library of Congress Cataloging-in-Publication Data
Names: Trapani, Iza, authors, illustrators.
Title: Old MacDonald had a . . . zoo? / Iza Trapani.
Description: Watertown, MA : Charlesbridge, [2017] | Summary: In this revision of the
    classic song, Farmer MacDonald finds his farm invaded by a kangaroo, an elephant,
    and other animals that belong to the zoo, until he rounds them up and takes them
    back where they belong.
Identifiers: LCCN 2016043037 (print) | LCCN 2016045157 (ebook) |
    ISBN 9781580897297 (reinforced for library use) |
    ISBN 9781607349730 (ebook) | ISBN 9781607349747 (ebook pdf)
Subjects: LCSH: Folk songs, English—United States—Texts. | Zoo animals—Juvenile
    fiction. | Farm life—Juvenile fiction. | CYAC: Folk songs—United States. | Zoo
    animals—Songs and music. | Farm life—Songs and music.
Classification: LCC PZ8.3.T686 Op 2017 (print) | LCC PZ8.3.T686 (ebook) | DDC
782.42 [E]—dc23
LC record available at https://lccn.loc.gov/2016043037

Printed in China
(hc) 10 9 8 7 6 5 4 3 2 1

Illustrations done in watercolor, Acryla gouache, ink, and colored pencil
    on Arches 140-lb. cold-pressed watercolor paper
Display type set in Badger by Red Rooster Typefounders
Text type set in Amasis by the Monotype Corporation
Color separations by Colourscan Print Co Pte Ltd, Singapore
Printed by 1010 Printing International Limited in Huizhou, Guangdong, China
Production supervision by Brian G. Walker
Designed by Diane M. Earley

Old MacDonald had a farm, **E-I-E-I-O**,
And on that farm he had a cow, **E-I-E-I-O**.
With a *moo moo* here, and a *moo moo* there,
Here a *moo*, there a *moo*,
Everywhere a *moo moo*,
Old MacDonald had a farm, **E-I-E-I-O**.

Old MacDonald in the sty, E-I-E-I-O,
Saw a kangaroo hop by, E-I-E-I-O.

With a *hop hop* up, and a *hop hop* down,
Here a *hop*, there a *hop*,
Everywhere a *hop hop*,
Mucky mud went flying high, **E-I-E-I-O**.

Old MacDonald heard a plunk, E-I-E-I-O.
An elephant had come to dunk, E-I-E-I-O.

With a *squirt squirt* near, and a *squirt squirt* far,
Here a *squirt*, there a *squirt*,
Everywhere a *squirt squirt*,
Water spurted from its trunk, **E-I-E-I-O**.

Old MacDonald heard a crunch, **E-I-E-I-O**.
Zebras helped themselves to lunch, **E-I-E-I-O**.

With a *chomp* above, and a *chomp* below,

Here a *chomp*, there a *chomp*,

Everywhere a *chomp chomp*,

What a hungry, messy bunch, **E-I-E-I-O**.

Old MacDonald gaped and frowned, E-I-E-I-O,
At monkeys swinging all around, E-I-E-I-O.

With a *whoosh whoosh* low, and a *whoosh whoosh* high,
Here a *whoosh*, there a *whoosh*,
Everywhere a *whoosh whoosh*,
Oops! The eggs fell on the ground, **E-I-E-I-O**.

Old MacDonald shook with fear, **E-I-E-I-O**,
When a crocodile came near, **E-I-E-I-O**.

With a *snap* to the front, and a *snap* to the back,
Here a *snap*, there a *snap*,
Everywhere a *snap snap*,
Everybody disappeared, E-I-E-I-O.

Old MacDonald cried, "No more!" **E-I-E-I-O**.

He stomped his foot hard on the floor, **E-I-E-I-O**.

With a *stomp stomp* left, and a *stomp stomp* right,

Here a *stomp*, there a *stomp*,

Everywhere a *stomp stomp*,

Now he had just one more chore, **E-I-E-I-O**.

Old MacDonald yelled, "We're through!" E-I-E-I-O.
In his trailer went the crew, E-I-E-I-O.

With a *vroom* to start, and a *vroom* to end,

Here a *vroom*, there a *vroom*,

Everywhere a *vroom vroom*,

He returned them to the zoo, **E-I-E-I-O**.

Zoo ahead

Old MacDonald Had a Farm

Old Mac-Don-ald had a farm, E - I - E - I - O, And on that farm he had a cow, E - I - E - I - O. With a

moo moo here, and a *moo moo* there, Here a *moo*, there a *moo*, Eve-ry-where a *moo moo*, Old Mac-Don-ald had a farm, E - I - E - I - O.

Old MacDonald in the sty, E-I-E-I-O,
Saw a kangaroo hop by, E-I-E-I-O.
With a *hop hop* up, and a *hop hop* down,
Here a *hop*, there a *hop*,
Everywhere a *hop hop*,
Mucky mud went flying high, E-I-E-I-O.

Old MacDonald heard a plunk, E-I-E-I-O.
An elephant had come to dunk, E-I-E-I-O.
With a *squirt squirt* near, and a *squirt squirt* far,
Here a *squirt*, there a *squirt*,
Everywhere a *squirt squirt*,
Water spurted from its trunk, E-I-E-I-O.

Old MacDonald heard a crunch, E-I-E-I-O.
Zebras helped themselves to lunch, E-I-E-I-O.
With a *chomp* above, and a *chomp* below,
Here a *chomp*, there a *chomp*,
Everywhere a *chomp chomp*,
What a hungry, messy bunch, E-I-E-I-O.

Old MacDonald gaped and frowned, E-I-E-I-O,
At monkeys swinging all around, E-I-E-I-O.
With a *whoosh whoosh* low, and a *whoosh whoosh* high,
Here a *whoosh*, there a *whoosh*,
Everywhere a *whoosh whoosh*,
Oops! The eggs fell on the ground, E-I-E-I-O.

Old MacDonald shook with fear, E-I-E-I-O,
When a crocodile came near, E-I-E-I-O.
With a *snap* to the front, and a *snap* to the back,
Here a *snap*, there a *snap*,
Everywhere a *snap snap*,
Everybody disappeared, E-I-E-I-O.

Old MacDonald cried, "No more!" E-I-E-I-O.
He stomped his foot hard on the floor, E-I-E-I-O.
With a *stomp stomp* left, and a *stomp stomp* right,
Here a *stomp*, there a *stomp*,
Everywhere a *stomp stomp*,
Now he had just one more chore, E-I-E-I-O.

Old MacDonald yelled, "We're through!" E-I-E-I-O.
In his trailer went the crew, E-I-E-I-O.
With a *vroom* to start, and a *vroom* to end,
Here a *vroom*, there a *vroom*,
Everywhere a *vroom vroom*,
He returned them to the zoo, E-I-E-I-O.